"I wish I had had this bo   .il-
dren were growing up; I think it would have saved a lot
of heartache for my whole family. Michael's words are
insightful; easy to put into immediate practice. Her advice is so logical that one wonders why one didn't think
of it herself. I will recommend this book to my patients
who are parents."

Jacqueline Parker PA-C,
Physicians Assistant and parent

"*Nitty Gritty Parenting* is written with pragmatic, sensible,
loving solutions to issues that every parent faces in their
daily interactions with children. Michael Aiello's important contribution is a beautiful book of parenting,
communication skills, and boundary setting that factor
in the best possible outcome for all. Written with vision,
experience, and tried and true methods that really work,
Michael provides the much needed depth and insight that
any parent can begin instantly implementing in the home.
Her sound advice builds a strong foundation for better re-
lations where feelings of harmony and safety are secured.
This valuable resource couldn't come at a better time."

Nell Arnaud, B.A.,
Elementary School Educator

"Michael Aiello has translated years of academic educational research into an experienced-based book for people who can use it the most; *parents.* Nitty gritty. Practical. Realistic. Helpful."

Catherine Lewis, M.A.,
Early Childhood Education

"I have personally witnessed Michael Aiello's ability to help children and their parents transform their lives for the last twenty years in the school setting. Michael is ALWAYS able to help. She has the unique ability to help children and their parents to see the positive aspects of their feelings and actions and where they may have originated, and to use that awareness to find more effective solutions to their challenges. I am elated that Michael has written this book, as more parents and children will be able to navigate through life with skills that will launch them into more loving and respectful relationships. The world is a better place because of Michael and her wisdom — and this book will keep that going."

Terri Sternberg, M.S.
K-8 Elementary School Teacher

"A must-read for parents. This book is simply written and goes deep into issues facing families everywhere. It is current, spunky, wise and hopeful."

Janet M. Bruce,
Former Educator and Marriage
& Family Therapist

MICHAEL AIELLO

Nitty Gritty
PARENTING

*A Practical Guide for Navigating
the Challenges of Parenting*

ISBN: 1451581963

ISBN-13: 9781451581966

Library of Congress Control Number: 2010904770

To my rising stars,
Cary, Cameron, Ashley, and Tessa

Table Of Contents

SECTION V: DEEPER WATERS

SECTION VI: COMING UP FOR AIR

Acknowledgements

Many thanks to my readers; my dear, gentle sister-friend, Terri Sternberg, and soul-kin, Dorian Aiello, for your keen eyes and great ideas. You both made Nitty Gritty Parenting a better book.

I acknowledge my fellow members in the Artist Conference Network, for your skilled coaching, positive feedback, friendship, laughter, and great food. Without the structure of the organization, my book would not be.

I am ever so grateful for my deep connection with my dearest gal pals, whose friendship and sisterhood sustain me on a daily basis.

I acknowledge the wonderful mentors I have been fortunate enough to have had along my path, most notably, my dear sister-friend, The Great Lonnie Mook, whose unique vision opened my eyes.

Hearty thanks to all of you I have worked with in the schools. Your dedication to children and your friendships are dear to me.

To the families who entrust me with the weave of their relationships and the psyches of their precious children; thank you for your courage to be the best parent you can be and for your faith in me.

To all you children who have visited me when you have had a problem or concern and who greet me in the halls with such great enthusiasm; you bless me with your love and trust. Thank you.

And then there are my children. My four daughters who are The Four Directions of my life; Cary, Cameron, Ashley, and Tessa. You have taught me the most about relationship and love. I love you so deeply and revel in the unique, wonderful, wild women you have grown into.

Thank you, Ms. Ashley Barnard, for your knowledge of and great guidance in the literary world of agents, publishers, and know-how. Good luck on your new book, *Shadow Fox*, (through Champagne Publishing).

Thank you, Cary and Cameron, for including me so lovingly in your family lives; and a special mention to my four sons-in-law who are always so welcoming when I come for a visit. And to my wonderful grandchildren, Cassie, Mark (and Jen!), Jordan, Spencer, Nick, Carson, Noah, Alexandria, Logan, Paige, and the little one on the way; thank you for being in my life. I love you all so much!

Thank you, Tessa, for the sweet gift of my web-site and for our wonderful walks and your support as I chattered incessantly about this book.

To the wild and wacky, sprawling Blankenship family and those relationships I have not yet mentioned that touch my heart. Many thanks.

Blessings to those who wrote such great testimonials. Thank you.

And thank you Doc Sternberg for keeping me and mine healthy.

Introduction

Nitty Gritty Parenting is a helping guide intended for parents to better understand how to parent from the positive spectrum; how relationships can become derailed; where the pratfalls lay and how to rescue a relationship drifting toward or submerged in negative waters. This book includes the psychological processes that can cause havoc with even the most positive intentions of a parent.

The major writings in this book are based on the problems that children and parents come to me with the most often. Imbedded in the writings are the workable solutions and an insightful look at the underpinnings of relationship.

Section I: *Inner Workings*, takes an in-depth look at recognizing and changing our own deeply-embedded childhood patterns that often dictate how we will respond to our child's behavior. Thankfully, there are ways to unravel the patterning to allow us to parent the way we always intended.

Section II: *Positive Communication*, is a pragmatic and detailed account of how to set up consequences with positive energy, how to use the tool of *validation*, and how to keep the communication open during touchy situations.

Section III: *Keeping it Positive*, creates a positive stance from which to parent, including how to dismantle a negative cycle, and how to communicate at an even deeper level.

Section IV: *The Teen Factor*, looks at the shifts in perception that our children experience as they transform into teenagers, how societal prejudice against teens can impact the relationship between parent and teenager, how parents can get knocked off the beloved pedestal, and how to set firm, and yet, loving boundaries.

Section V: *Deeper Waters* dives into the scariest aspects of parenting; the warning signs of depression/suicidal thinking, the impact of domestic violence on the children, and how the psyche expresses itself through behavior and physical/emotional symptoms.

Section VI: *Coming up for Air*, bobs back up to more manageable levels as it looks at the impact of scary movies and scary news on the psyche, the benefits of giving children choices, and how to curb the complaining factor.

The intention of the teachings and tools provided in each chapter, when gathered as a whole and generalized to the broader aspects of parenting, is to provide an insightful, compassionate, confident, and loving platform from which to parent.

SECTION I

INNER WORKINGS

Taken Hostage

If, when you were little, you got yelled at for spilling your milk, for example, or received a strapping for telling a lie, these charged incidences were introjected* (implanted) into your psyche. In other words, the scenes were stored in your psyche like a two reeled film clip. The more times you were yelled at for spilling your milk, the more substantial the reel, or patterning. The one reel is you receiving the verbal or physical punishment. The other reel is your parent doling out that punishment. These two reels are stored deep into your psyche, along with the emotional field of both you and amazingly, of your parent.

Meanwhile, you grew up and life moved on. The inner reels began to collect psychic dust and became

---

* Note: Introjection and Projection are psychological concepts developed by Freud.

covered with shadowy vines. Possibly you made decisions about how you would parent differently, and then did, until one day, your child reaches the age you were when you began getting into trouble for the spilled milk. And then it happens; she/he accidentally knocks over a glass of milk. In this moment, the possibility is great that this incident will trigger the dormant reels into action. If, all of a sudden you feel an uncalled for rage for such a trivial incident, you have just been taken hostage by the introject of your parent, and as the reel runs, you become the unwitting projector. The stored scenes jump to life and your child becomes the backdrop of the first reel, and the symbol or stand-in, for your inner child. Dread words begin to fly out of your mouth; the very ones you swore you would never utter, as the stored memory and the stored emotional state of your parent, speak through you.

The first born, same sex child is most likely the child that will become the back-drop of the projection because of the similarity to you when you were a child. But other similarities, such as looks, attitude, or behaviors that mirror the inner reel are also triggers. The emotional charge of the incident when you were little is what created the patterning in the first place, and the patterning is triggered by similar incidents when you are parenting your child.

There is hope here. There are ways to unravel the patterning to allow you to parent the way you always intended. Understanding the dynamic is the first step.

Tip: If you feel rage toward your child you are most likely caught up in the web of projection. Since your child, at this moment, is a stand in for your inner child, there is a healing potential for you both.

Unraveling The Reels
Of Patterning

U nderstanding the basics of introjection and projection, is the first step in unraveling or re-patterning the inner reels. The second step requires setting the stage in advance. Now that you understand, i.e., that your child's spilled milk can trigger the stored psychic reels into action, you will need to rehearse in your mind many times what you will do the next time that glass teeters onto the table cloth. By doing this you are creating etchings of a new pattern and an alternate route to take when the dormant reels come to life. Remember, the old pattern has deep grooves and jumps to life with a charged emotional field. Since the charged emotional field is the glue that holds the reel together, you will be standing in the center of an emotional lake when your child inadvertently triggers the reels into action.

So, let's say, that you decide that when next your child spills the milk, you will casually get up and walk into another room or go outside and just stand back for a minute and feel the magnitude of the take-over. Actually, the farther away from your child the better, because the emotional field that envelopes you will be huge and the pattern's pull is powerful. As you focus on the stunning dynamic of the emotional kidnapping from your introjected parent, you have just shifted the patterning in two ways:

1). You left the scene without allowing the introject to speak through you.

2). You felt the emotional field from the *Observer* view point rather than from the *Projective* one. In other words you observed the huge emotion racking you without directing it at your child. Once you realize the dynamic is within you and it is not really about your child, the shift in the patterning is already taking place.

But there you are, still outside and "reeling" from the shock of the force of the patterning. Stay focused on the emotional field from the perspective of the

Observer, until you feel it dissipate down to nothing. Then go back to the table with a rag to mop the milk up, and say to your child something like, "No problem." Be prepared for your child to look frightened and to be clumsy in his/her panic (that's why *you* need to mop up the mess and not them unless they have already done it in your absence). The last thing either one of you need is for your child to accidentally spill anything else as they mop up, thereby triggering the reels back into action.

If you successfully do this, you have just created new patterning grooves that overlay the old deep ones. The more times you are successful, the deeper the grooves, until you won't need to go outside anymore. The deeper the new positive patterning, the more you unravel the old negatively charged one. One day your child will spill the milk and you will keep on chattering about the flowers in the back yard without skipping a beat, and you will be able to smile lovingly at your little one, and feel the grace descend upon you and your child *and* your inner child as three are healed in one.

Tip: Obviously, only some parents get triggered by spilled milk. Whatever the trigger is for you, the action is the same. Go outside or into another room before you let the pattern have its way and then let the emotional field die down before you return. Remember, the patterning was locked in by the emotional field, and so that means you must do something differently than your parent did while you are in that emotional field in order to unlock it. You can explain later to your child why you abruptly left the room, if you feel the need.

Making Reparation

Okay, so you blew it. Dread words flew out before you could get outside. Remember that the old patterning is powerful and at first, when you are working on changing the patterns, if you even so much as open your mouth, the pattern will seize you. That is why you have to leave immediately when you feel you are about to be taken hostage.

What you do next is important. If you go to your child when things are calm and tell them you are sorry for what was said and that you are working on shifting an old negative pattern from your childhood, you have begun the process of reparation (repairing the damage). This sounds simple, but it is profound. Imagine what it would have been like for you as a child if your parent came to you after such an incident and told you they were so sorry and that they were actively working on not doing that anymore; and further told you that this dynamic was about them when they were a child and really not about you. What a release that would have been for you. What a notion that it wasn't about you being bad or worthless, but that you were just a hapless trigger. What a profound relief. If you do that for your child you also accomplish:

- The shifting of the pattern simply by doing something differently than your parent did.

- You undo a lot of the damage just done.

- There will be a healing for your child, and therefore, also, for your inner child. Remember, in patterning, your child is a stand-in for your inner child. When you parent your child the way you wanted and needed to be parented, there is an immediate healing to your inner child and therefore to you in the present time. You can once again feel the grace descend upon you, your child, and your inner child.

In all fairness, you can tell your child what it is that they inadvertently do that triggers the old patterning. You two could possibly put your heads together to figure out how to avoid or soften the triggers. For example, in the spilled milk scenario, a fat, squat, heavy, tumbler for the milk might do the trick to make it more difficult for your child to spill their milk. Get creative. However, if triggered, take responsibility and head for the hills.

> **Tip:** When projecting, one actually creates the situation to fit the patterning. For example, if your child gets in trouble for spilling the milk, she/he will become frightened about spilling the milk in the future. That preoccupation and focus on not spilling the milk, works like a magnet. And then of course, in all likelihood, the milk will spill all the more often. Your child will become clumsy in her/his panic, but not clumsy by nature. And, voila, the "perfect" situation is created to allow the reels to run unhindered.

> **Tip #2:** Another thing that allows the reels to run unhindered is too much alcohol. When people are punch drunk they are running on unconscious content. In other words, those psychic inner reels are running wildly with no stoppers. That's why there is so much havoc reaped during an alcohol binge.

Complexes Are The Pits

Complexes* are an important aspect of how reality is, at times, viewed through a biased filter. They are part of the makeup of our unconscious mind and are formed by traumatic interrelated incidents which are introjected into the psyche, creating a significant psychic wound. The emotional overwhelm which flooded the mind and body at the time of each traumatic incident is also introjected into the psyche, for example, feelings of shame, unworthiness, rage, etc. These charged emotional states cluster around the psychic wound, acting like a beacon or homing device and gather to the wound any related traumatic material in the future.

So let's say that when you were a child, you had a parent or caregiver who repeatedly told you, in one

---

* Note: Theodore Ziehen is credited with coining the term, Complex, in 1898. Both Freud and Jung use the concept in their psychological systems.

way or another, that you were stupid. This would create a wound that would be reinforced by more and more repetitions and more and more emotional flooding.

Let's also say that when you were little you started to doubt your intellectual integrity because you were always being told at home that you were not intelligent. Hence, at school, the self-doubt would begin to creep in and, perhaps, your academic performance would begin to suffer. Due to this, perhaps other children either maliciously or unintentionally, might let you know that they felt you were lacking "upstairs." As you felt their judgment, and became flooded with more shame, these additional traumatic experiences, including the emotional field, would be introjected to the site of the original wound, creating a *complex*; a complexity of interrelated psychic traumas gathered at one site.

If you could imagine the wound in the shape of a large pit that you could fall into, and that as you fell, you would be greeted by every other related incident that created and reinforced the pit, along with the release of the stored emotional states that awaited you, and in fact guided you, you would get a sense of how powerful and all consuming a complex can be.

Once in the pit, or complex, all you would be able to see would be the things that reinforce its creation. The only things that exist in this pit are the traumatic incidents that support it and the traumatic emotional glue that holds it together. In other words, this is not a holistic picture of reality. It is the reality of the wound only. When people fall into a complex, they are seeing from the limited view of the pit, they are flooded with all the stored emotional material, and in the reality of the wound/complex/pit, the only things that exist there, are the things that support the wound.

So let's say that when you grow up, your co-worker gets the promotion you were hoping for. It might be because of seniority, or because the co-worker is more aligned for the position, or her personality is better suited for the job. And let's say that the boss feels you are super capable and has you in mind for the next promotion. However, because of the nature of the complex, in all probability, you would plunge head over heals deeply into the wound, and know, without a doubt, that your boss thinks you aren't intelligent enough for the job. You would know this without a doubt. And in this case, you would be wrong.

As you can already foresee, there are so many incidents in life that not only could trigger the painful plunge back into the complex, but in fact could reinforce it with new material, even if that material was misinterpreted. Complexes just aren't picky.

In one such incident, perhaps you are home one night and your teen needs help with their homework. The homework is getting more and more complicated with a crazy new math, or advanced algebra that you have forgotten over the years from non-use. However, as you realize that you can't help your teen, and as feelings of inadequacy arise, which are related to the complex, you may find yourself doing another back flip into the pit. Your teen didn't need to do anything but just ask for help. When you land in the complex, however, you will be flooded with many emotional states, all of them pointing to the anguish of being made to feel stupid by others. You may simply start beating yourself up internally about how stupid you are that you can't even figure out how to do your child's homework. However, if your teen is unfortunate enough at this moment to be glib, and say something like, "What's the matter, can't you figure it out? What did they teach you in school?", then they best make a run for it, for Mt. Vesuvius is about to erupt. In truth, they may get splattered anyway, even if they say nothing.

Since complexes are created in our psyches from interrelated traumatic incidents, your children will most likely eventually develop some of their own. When they are speaking from one of their complexes, they will also know they are right, even when they have jagged left.

Tip: When you or your child are in a complex, you or she/he can only see a one-sided picture of reality. The picture is of the traumatic incidents that reinforce the complex and the traumatic emotional glue that holds it together. Nothing else exists there. None of the wonderful things that you have done for each other exist there; only the things that support the wound.

CRAWLING OUT OF THE PIT

The first steps in crawling out of a complex are:

- The prior knowledge that complexes exist.

- Knowing what kind of situation sends you spinning into a complex.

- Knowing when you are, indeed, smack in the middle of the complex.

When people go into emotional overwhelm and come up shooting from the hip, either at themselves (imploding) or at another (exploding) over incidences that have a common theme, i.e., situations that trigger feelings of abandonment, or resentment toward authority figures, or feelings of inadequacy, chances are they have located their complex. The types of complexes are numerous and vary according to each person and his or her life history.

Once one starts ferreting out situations that trigger a response of emotional overwhelm, he or she may begin to see a relationship between those triggers; triggers that lead to the same wound. If someone were abandoned when they were young and also had feelings of inadequacy about their intellect, they could very well have two different complexes, and so some triggers would lead to one wound, and other triggers would lead to another.

But let's go back to the scenario from Complexes Are The Pits that when you were a child you had a parent or caregiver who repeatedly told you that you were not so smart. So, here you are all grown up now and you are with your teen while they are asking, once again, for help with their homework; that blasted new math. If you know that complexes exist, and you have ferreted out your sensitivities regarding feelings of inadequacy, let's say, then you already know that the potential is great that you will be triggered in this situation. If, indeed, you can't make heads or tails out of the homework assignment, and your teen gets impatient, not because they feel you aren't capable but maybe because they have a cute someone they want to go see, you may be well on your way to falling backward into the pit. You'll know when you land there, because you will be flooded with strong emotional states. If, when that happens, you leave the room and start to tell yourself, *"I am in a complex.... my vision is clouded... I don't need to do anything... these feelings will pass,"* then you are well on your way to finding the footholds out of the pit. Just keep walking; going outside is good if it is feasible, and keep telling yourself that you are in a complex. You will have accomplished several things:

- When you landed in the complex, you brought with you the tools to crawl out:

  - The knowledge that you are in a complex

  - The knowledge that your perception is distorted while in the complex.

- By walking away and telling yourself that you are in a complex, you are not reinforcing the wound by adding a new trauma, in fact you are adding something unique and powerful to the complex: *insight*.

- Your teen didn't get splattered with righteous indignation, and the relationship between you two didn't get compromised.

Tip: Once you come to know your complex well, and can see how one-sided its vision is, you can make a list for yourself that includes all the things that the complex leaves out, for example, how capable you are, or all the wonderful things your spouse does that you can't remember when you are in a complex about him or her. This will be very handy the next time you find yourself doing a back flip into the pit. As you crawl your way out with your newly learned skills, you can go to your list and see the greater truth of who you are and of those around you. As you bring new tools and insight into the complex, you change its makeup and begin to reduce its potency. Halleluiah. Well done!

SECTION II

POSITIVE COMMUNICATION

SETTING UP CONSEQUENCES
WITH POSITIVE ENERGY

onsequences are not the same as punishments.
Punishment carries with it negative energy; a
sense of *you are in trouble now!* It comes from the
stance of being whipped into shape, rather than guided
toward positive choices. Punishment may get an immediate response, but it also creates an emotional de-
tour between the initial cause and its consequence. For
example, if children get *punished* for bad grades, instead
of gaining the wisdom that bad grades get in the way of
success, the experience is instead, many times, interpret-
ed as: "my parents don't care about me; they only care
about my grades." This in turn can launch a negative
cycle as your child's understanding of the dynamic could

lead to passive/aggressive behavior; "If all my parents care about are my grades, then I won't get good grades."

Other times the fear of the punishment itself can cause a panic that interferes with the brain's functioning and therefore good grades become more difficult to attain. If children fear punishment, it also can set up a dynamic of *telling tall tales* in order to escape the wrath of a parent. Now the relationship between parent and child is compromised and a negative cycle has been set in motion.

Setting up consequences with positive energy is a way of holding children accountable as they are taught the natural laws of cause and effect and how one creates their own reality. There is no negative energy introduced into the equation to derail the learning or compromise the relationship.

In order to set up consequences with positive energy:

• Meet with your child during a calm period.

• Discuss the problem behavior and the need for compliance.

• Enlist your child in helping set up a consequence.

• Choose a consequence that is doable for your child and for yourself, and which is appropriate.

Consequences are effective when set up ahead of time, when your child is involved with setting them up, and when the consequence is something she or he cares about. You want a consequence that will motivate your child, but not traumatize them.

• When a plan is reached, shake hands to formalize the contract. For example, if one of your child's chores is taking out the garbage at night and they keep putting off the chore and it drives you crazy, then the plan could be that your child will take out the garbage every night by 7:00 p.m., and if they are late, even for one minute, then the consequence of, let's say, missing their favorite TV show that night, will automatically kick in.

• Assume your child will fulfill their end of the contract; this will help them feel responsible and trustworthy, and hence, will further motivate them. For example, after you shake hands to lock in the deal, if you say something like, "Oh, I'm so glad we figured *that* out, now I don't have to worry about it anymore," they will realize that you take their word and their problem solving skills seriously. They will want then, in all likelihood, to be that trustworthy person you have just identified them to be.

- If it looks like your child is *about* to "blow it," align with him/her in becoming successful. For example, if you notice there are only 5 minutes before the agreed upon deadline to take out the garbage, and you can see they are engrossed in another activity, you can say something like, "Oh no! You are going to miss your favorite program!" This kind of statement shows empathy and infers that the consequence is out of *your* hands now; that it is bigger than the two of you because of the *Contract* that was made. When they see you are rooting for them to be successful and that you are truly empathetic about the possibility that they might miss their program, you have just landed in the position of the *Cheerleader* for their success, rather than that of the *Heavy* or the *Enforcer*. Ultimately, however, it is your child's responsibility to fulfill their end of the contract. It is not up to you to remind them daily, but as the contract is first implemented, it is a graceful way of grounding the reality of the contract, as well as the opportunity for you to show your child that you are working with them and not against them.

- If your child has already blown it, be empathetic that she/he is going to miss out on something they care about. Again, act as if the consequence has its own power now. Resist throwing negative, angry, punitive, or mocking energy into the mix (even if the unwanted behavior is crazy making or pushes your buttons). If they are two minutes late in the example of taking out the garbage, say something like, "Oh no! Oh, you were so close!!! I know tomorrow you will get the job done on time!" If they beg to watch the program because they were so close, you can say, "I'm sorry, I can't break the contract! However, I have great faith in you that you will get the job done tomorrow before deadline and that you will get to see your program!" In all probability, they *will* have the job done the next night before deadline!

If you make a contract about something that will take children a great deal of time to complete, have the deadline be the *starting point* of the project, and when they finish they can then go to the park or to the movies, or whatever it is you two have agreed upon. You don't want to set them up for failure, by having them work on something all day, which they potentially can't finish by deadline.

- Remember to load on positive reinforcement for the positive behaviors your child displays. The more positive you are, the more positive your child will be. If you focus on negative behaviors, so will your child.

• Focus on the positive and have consequences in place for the unwanted behaviors.

• Remember to talk about your child's good points and not their negative ones, when you talk about them in their presence. The way you talk about them, gives them a sense of who they are. If you talk about how difficult they are, they will decide that is, indeed, who they are, and they will become even more difficult.

• With positive reinforcement, setting up consequences for unwanted behaviors, adding your loving energy, and talking about your child in positive ways, your child has the ability to be successful and you and your child have the ability to maintain a positive, intimate relationship.

Tip: Remember to agree on a consequence that you can live with. Once you shake on a deal, it becomes a contract. Therefore, you don't want to put yourself in a position where you might regret setting it up or where you can't bear to see your child live out the consequence. If you break a contract because, for instance, you can't stand to see your child miss out on the park, and you say something like, "just this once," they will now see that one's word isn't necessarily gold. What you are trying to teach your child is to be responsible, to stand by their word, to let them recognize the direct link between cause and effect. If you don't honor the contract, neither will they. All further contracts, including the one you just made, won't be taken seriously. Your child will recognize that there are loop holes to the contracts, and their focus will be on finding those holes, rather than striving to fulfill the contract. If you don't keep up your end of the contract, this will turn into a crazy making situation for you!

VALIDATION

Validation is one of the hallmarks of open communication. For example, if your teen comes to you and says, "Starting a new job is so hard!" If you agree with your teen and say, "Those first two weeks are killers," your validation has just launched the conversation and your child feels perfectly understood and will feel safe in sharing with you what is so daunting for her/him on the new job. The more you validate what is shared, the deeper the conversation will go, and the more aligned your teen will feel with you, which opens the door for them to come to you in the future with other problems because you demonstrated to them that you are open, present, understanding, non-judgmental, and helpful. All begun from one little validation.

Now, if your first remark was, "*I* love starting new jobs! No problem for *me!*" You can see that the conversation would have jogged left. Your child would be more apt to clam up because they wouldn't feel that you would understand, and, sadly, it would leave them dangling in mid-trouble. Even if it were true that you did love starting new jobs, that really wasn't at the heart of the fledgling conversation. At the heart was that your teen was having difficulties and needed help processing those difficulties. At the very least, they needed a good ear. So if it were true that you did love starting new jobs, but still wanted to validate their perspective, then simply summarizing their position would do the trick; something like, "Uh Oh, things don't sound like they are going so well." Once again you launched the conversation into the possibility of deeper territory where you now have the opportunity to throw in jewels of wisdom that can help your child. Even if there are no jewels of wisdom to be shared in a given situation, just accompanying your teen on their journey into their confusion and fear is quite enough.

Back to the opening statement of, "Starting a new job is so hard!" If you had said, "*What* did you do now!!??" Guess where that conversation is going to go. Closed down. Locked up. Key thrown in the bushes. Retreating backside. Next time they are in trouble they will most likely go find another ear, and that would be quite unfortunate, because no one loves your child more than you, and you have worlds of wisdom to pass on to them.

Validation goes a long way:

- It honors your child's perspective

- It gives your child the feeling of being listened to, understood, and aligned with.

- It allows for talking it out, instead of acting it out.

- It gives you the opportunity to:

  - get a feel for your child's reality

  - dissolve your child's and your defenses

  - establish a deeper intimacy

  - help problem solve

  - ease in some jewels of wisdom

- It avoids negative outcome by:

  - side-stepping a power struggle

- cooling down a hot situation

- not blaming

- not stripping your child of their power and dignity

• It is a key component for building positive relationships.

• It builds character (especially yours, if you are being challenged).

• It keeps the door open for next time.

Tip: If you validate your child and withhold judgment, you will most likely be invited into their world where you have the opportunity to drop pearls of wisdom and be a beloved guide as they journey down their life's path.

OPEN COMMUNICATION
DURING TOUCHY SITUATIONS

If your child comes to you with a problem that has the potential of distressing you, try to focus only on what *they* are saying; not what *you* are saying in your head. If the problem triggers a feeling of emotional overwhelm in you, and you recognize you are about to fall into a complex (refer to Complexes Are the Pits) or that you are about to be taken hostage by the negative patterns from your childhood (refer to Taken Hostage), then signal to them you'll get back with them as soon as possible. Don't attempt to communicate with them beyond that, until the emotional overwhelm has vanished. When you are calm let your child know that you are ready to listen and help them through this period of their life.

But let's begin with a simpler problem. Let's say they got into trouble at school:

- Stay neutral, suspend judgment.

- Ask what happened, listen for areas that you can help them with later.

- Try to step into their shoes, to see it from their perspective.

- Don't blame or shame.

- Help them to problem solve so they can avoid the same pit fall in the future.

- formulate a workable plan.

Now let's say that they come home and they are once again in trouble at school:

- Ask them what went wrong with the plan.

- Listen for the areas where the plan fell apart.

- Come up with a new plan.

At school, there will already be consequences in place, for example, missed recess, detention, the inability to participate in reward parties; things of this nature. At this point you get to be the problem solver rather than the *Enforcer*; the wiser eyes to assess the situation and help your child see the circumstances more holistically. However, if the situation continues, you may need to get to the school and problem solve with the teacher *and* your child, so that all parties are present and you get the full understanding of the problem. If the problem continues and you feel it is because your child isn't "putting in" to make the plan work, then you have a couple of choices:

1) You can draw attention to the reality your child is creating (missing recess, getting detention, etc.) by saying something like, "Huh! You must not like recess." Or, "Do you have a cute classmate in detention, because you keep landing yourself there?" Or, "Your choices are interesting to me; they make me think that you enjoy getting into trouble more than you enjoy going to recess." This creates the link for them to know that their actions are responsible for the consequences and that it has nothing to do with their teacher being mean or that they are getting picked on.

2) If you feel the consequences at school aren't working, you can sit with your child and create a contract (refer to Setting Up Consequences) so that the stakes are

higher. Remember to not give any negative energy to the process, because it could potentially create an emotional roadblock for your child between the link of cause and effect.

As your child recognizes how open, calm, and validating you are when they find themselves in choppy waters, they will most likely continue to come to you when they have troubles. As your child gets older their troubles can get more complicated and they will need your counsel all the more. Very difficult situations can arise as your child grows up. Some teens have to face pregnancy, peer pressure to drink and/or use drugs, or other issues that can create despondency. Remember the steps:

- stay neutral; suspend judgment.

- ask how they got into the situation; listen for areas that you can help them with.

- step into their shoes; try to understand their world.

- don't blame or shame them.

- help them to problem solve.

- formulate a workable plan.

The more difficult the issues, the more difficult the plans. Hopefully you and your child will never have to navigate these more difficult waters, but if you do, they will give thanks that you are there helping to steer them to safety.

Tip: When communication stays open during touchy situations, the potential is great that your child will come to rely on your wise counsel, and seek you out later when they are truly in great need.

SECTION III

KEEPING IT POSITIVE

CONNECTION IS EVERYTHING

E very time your child walks into the room or asks you a question, you have the opportunity to once again welcome them into your life.

If you *are* asked a question, and you look up (or down) and smile in anticipation, this tells your child that they are loved and a welcome part of your moment to moment life. If you are interrupted several times with questions, make light of it with a humorous face that gets them laughing but also makes the point that you need to concentrate on the task at hand.

If your little one interrupts you when you are on the phone, hold up a finger that says just a moment, and motion them over. When in reach, hold on to one of their fingers so they are grounded in the connection with you. After a minute, they will probably pull their finger out because they are impatient to get back to whatever they were doing, and they won't want to stand there all day. When they try to pull their finger out, gently hold on for a few seconds longer. This tells them their company is wanted and that is the reassurance they needed in the first place. The more you hold on, the faster they want to get away, and you have your phone conversation to yourself!

Tip: When your child tries to break a connection with you, hold on for a second longer. This fills them with the confidence that their company is precious to you and that they are valuable, lovable beings.

Tip #2: If you awaken your child in the morning lovingly, your connection with them starts off on a positive note and the world becomes something to look forward to. If they are heavy sleepers, awaken them gently and, if very young, guide them to the bathroom. If they are older and sound sleepers, set them up with an alarm clock across the room, so they become responsible for getting themselves up and resent the clock rather than you when it is time to get up. Awakening to positive energy sets a positive tone for the day.

CAN YOU HEAR ME NOW?

Cell phones are a very handy way of staying connected to your child when they are out and about. If your preteen is begging for a cell phone you are in the perfect position to benevolently say something like, "You know, this might be the perfect solution for me to know that you are safe when you are out with your friends." They will be so excited to get the phone, they will happily agree to the conditions. You can set up the cell phone conditions, for example, so that your preteen/teen will call you every two hours when they are out, and in this way you will know that all is well.

What a great opportunity for both of you.

The advantages of the two-hour check in are:

- Every two hours you can exhale and know that your child is safe.

- When your teen is older and more mobile they can keep you tuned in to their current where-a-bouts.

- Your teen knows they will be calling in every two hours and *talking* to you so they know they have to have it together enough to at least appear sober (don't set up the check-ins for texting because you will want to hear their voice to make sure they are alive, safe, and sober; anyone can text you on their phone, even someone with ulterior motives).

- The two hour check-ins give you the opportunity to give your child "on the job training" if a *situation* occurs. In other words, if they stop by a party and call you from there at the appointed time, you have an opportunity to be of guidance if there is a concern. For instance, let's say that your teen has been calling in for months now since you got them their "sweet" phone, and every time they call, you always sound glad to hear from them, and interested in what is going on in their outing. On their third call of this particular night, you answer, and say, "Now what's happening?" You sound interested, non-judgmental, and alert. So they tell you they (your teen and their friends) just found the big party in the pines. You can ask them if they feel safe. You can ask if anyone is in trouble. If they say, "You can't believe this!! Adam is stagger-ing around and is so wasted!" Then you have the opportunity to suggest that they help get Adam's keys away from him, and help get him home. Or if your teen says, "There are Freshman girls here, totally wasted" then you can ask your teen, "How can you help them before something happens to the girls?"

You can help your teen problem-solve; to become part of the solution, rather than part of the problem. They will be receiving on the job training from you on how to deal with a situation in the moment of impend-ing crisis, rather than not knowing what to do and let-ting disaster strike. As you help them problem solve in these real life situations as they are occurring, your teen will be developing their social conscience, they will be-come empowered, and view themselves as significant. As they get used to working out solutions with you during the check-ins, if there is a crisis at another time during the night and they don't know how to handle it, chances are they will call you for support.

- You become part of your teen's world. You will learn how they handle situations when they are not with you; you will begin to learn who is trustworthy in their world, and who they should be wary of.

- Your teen's friends will recognize you as a guide after many exchanges from your teen telling them something like, "Mom's asking how we can help the Freshman girls;" or, "Dad says we need to get the keys away from Adam;" and, hence, your teen's friends will feel comfortable coming to your house when the evening is over. When your teen walks in to excitedly tell you what else happened during the evening, so will her/his friends.

To keep this positive exchange going, remember:

- Always act glad to hear from your teen when they call in (if you act like it is a bother to talk to them when they call, then they will resent the need to call in, and will keep it as brief and distant as possible).

- Be the guide and not the judge (if you judge and lecture your teen when they call, they will withhold the truth of what is occurring during their evening out).

> **Tip:** The cell phone can be your link to your pre-teen/teen's world outside of home. It can beam you smack dab into the middle of their night out, in a healthy, hands-on way. Can you hear me now?

DO ONE BETTER

It is a good thing, the practice of warning your children when you have had a bad day. However, if you include your children in the healing process of your rotten day, rather than act as if their mere presence will be your breaking point, you have just done one better. I'm not talking about *parentifying* (acting as if your children are adults and burdening them with more than they can handle), but acting as if your children's presence and their ability to give love, will have a positive impact on your negative experiences of the day.

Warning your children says, "stay clear or I'll blow." *Including* your children, gives them the opportunity to rise to the occasion and says to them, "you are a safe haven," which, then, of course, makes them feel significant.

For example, if you come home after a bad day at work and say to your children, "I am *so* glad to be home, work was *horrible*; come give me hugs!" you have accomplished many things:

- You have informed your children that you are in a tender state.

- You have invited them in rather than keeping them out.

- You have made them part of the solution rather than part of the problem.

- You have made them feel significant.

- You have modeled an extremely positive response to stress.

It is amazing how nurturing children can be when given the opportunity. If you tell them your day was rotten and you want a hug, they'll not only hug you, but pat and croon, too.

If bickering breaks out between siblings while you are still in your fragile state, then tell them you are still recovering from your day and that *bickering* will send you over the edge. It is important that you say it is the bickering that is the problem and not them. If the bickering continues, or starts up again, say something like, "I need you to separate for an hour and play quietly so I can figure out what went wrong with my day today. Thank you so much."

> **Tip:** When you have had a bad day and you tell your children you are so glad to see their sweet faces, in an otherwise rotten day, they will surprise you by how comforting they can be. They will feel significant and the ensuing burst of love coming from them will be a healing balm.

POSITIVE/NEGATIVE CHARGE

Your children need your energy. If you don't have the time or the "energy" to give, they will extract it from you drop by drop. When it is extracted, it usually comes out in a negative form. However, if you give positive energy for positive action and no energy for negative action, your children will need to stay in the positive spectrum in order to get your energy. It works like this: If your children do something you don't like, just tell them that it's not OK with you. If the behavior continues, set up consequences, but in either event, don't throw any negative energy into the mix; don't flash anger, or get puffed up, or any of the other negative possibilities. Because your children need your energy, they will pipeline into whatever energy is available. Of course, your children would prefer positive energy, but when a parent is up against a deadline, too preoccupied, or having a bad day, children will settle for negative energy, which to them, is better than no energy.

If a parent is severely depressed, they have no energy to give. In a case such as this, their children could feel shunned or non-existent. Negative energy isn't the preferred drink of choice, however, it will do in a pinch to children who need to feel they exist; to feel they have an impact; to feel that they are in relationship.

When children settle for negative energy, they know they can elicit it over and over again if that is what they need to do to feel noticed. This, of course, sets up a negative cycle, for when children constantly misbehave, they magnetize negative energy. And so the cycle goes. However, if you begin to give only positive energy, children will be forced to move over to and hang out in the positive spectrum.

Therefore, when your children misbehave, give them no energy; *consequences*, yes; energy, no. When your children are behaving in ways that are appropriate and you wish the behaviors to continue, load on the positive energy. Remember, praise without energy is empty. Praise with positive energy carries with it smiles, gratitude, pride, and love, which feeds your children, and nourishes them in positive ways.

Save the "negative" energy for "show stoppers." For example, if your young child is running out into a busy street, that is when you yell, "STOP!" with all the energy behind it of danger and command. Dangerous situations call for immediate action, and if your child only hears your raised voice when danger is at hand, she/he will come to know that when you boom out a command, there is danger present, and hopefully, the response will be immediate.

Remember to give positive energy to your children not just for positive action, but also in the form of unconditional love. For example, as you walk by them, beam at them for no other reason except for the fact that you love them. Gather them into hugs and tell them how wonderful they are when they are just "being." This tells them that they are precious, not because of how they perform tasks, or how well they do in school, but just because they are who they are.

Tip: Since your children need your energy, if you only give them positive energy for positive action, and no energy for negative action, they will learn to hang out in the positive spectrum. When you give consequences for negative action don't add any negative energy into the mix (refer to Setting Up Consequences).

BUSTING A NEGATIVE CYCLE

There is little room left for doubt when you find yourself in a negative cycle with your child. Stink bombs keep landing at each other's feet in the form of eye rolling, door slamming, puffing up, threats, laden silences, and negative innuendo, just to name a few possibilities. It doesn't really matter who started the cycle rolling, since perspective is the inventor of reality. Hence, both parties in the negative cycle will point their finger at the other. Rather than grappling with your child toward the cliff's edge, your energy would be better spent in dismantling the cycle.

Dismantling a negative cycle is not about giving in or letting go of what you hold dear or deem moral. It's not about letting your child off the hook regarding account-ability or respect. A negative cycle, once started, generates a life of its own, and becomes so mired in resentment and outrage that notions such as accountability, cause and effect, and natural consequences are lost in the quagmire. For your child, the focus will be on the latest spear they feel has landed in their spleen. Remember, in a negative cycle, both parties are hurtling stink bombs in response to the belief that they were somehow wounded by the other. Many times the stink bombs the parents throw into the mix are simply the negative energies they launch along with consequences being doled out. Clean up the negative energies and the negative cycle begins to dissipate.

You can begin to turn around a negative cycle by doing small, simple, positive things and then building to the more complex, like:

- Kiss and Run. This is similar to hit and run, but with positive energy. For example, walk by your child and throw a compliment their way, or briefly, tenderly touch their shoulder from behind, and keep walking. Don't look back. You won't want to see the eye rolling, the shrug off, or whatever other negative reaction was waiting for you. Remember, a negative cycle gains momentum and it takes time to redirect it to the higher road.

- Do more of the above. This alone will start to diffuse the negativity. Your child will naturally start to match your energy as long as:

- You don't "put in" to the negative pot. If your child rolls their eyes or does whatever it is that triggers a negative response from you, just go on about your business. If it is something that requires consequences, like swearing at you or leaving the house and/or coming in late, then talk to them in a calm period and set up consequences with a problem solving attitude. Tell them something like, "Your swearing at me is not okay. Let's work out a way for you to convey your anger without the swearing." And when you reach a solution that is acceptable for both of you, then put consequences into place just in case swear words are unleashed the next time your child is angry with you. (Refer to Setting Up Consequences, which is a step by step guide in how to put consequences into place with positive energy).

However, a critical piece here is if you are setting up consequences for their swearing, and you swear at them when you are angry; then all bets are off, and the war will rage on. Remember, their sense of fair play is one of the standards that teens and preteens live by.

If they leave and/or come back late, let them know that that isn't okay with you and that it causes you to worry about them. This let's them know that you care about them and that you put rules into place for a reason related to your love for them rather than as a power play.

Remember, children are egocentric and so they need to be reminded about what motivates you, for example, love, fear, peace of mind, happiness. In a negative cycle they will *not* think you are motivated by love. They will see your anger and make their own assumptions and then fire a cannon shot in response.

After you let them know that you worry about them if they run off or are late, then problem solve with them about what consequences will motivate them and what you can both live with.

You want to teach your child about life and its consequences, but when negative energy is in the mix it derails and distracts them from the learning. Negative energy is a powerful force that severs the link between the natural rhythm of cause and effect. It sets up an emotional road block.

When things are running smoothly with you and your child, and your child displays an unwanted behavior, for example, coming in late, getting in trouble at school, or a drop in grades; if you say to your child, "That's an interesting choice," that teaches them that *they* are creating their reality. You don't have to be the *Heavy*, just be consistent. Meet with your child and problem solve with them; put consequences into place and honor the contract. If they break the contract, show empathy for the loss of privilege they are about to experience. This leaves the link between cause and effect unobstructed, and your child is able to experience that their actions in life have subsequent consequences.

Don't give any energy to things that irritate you about your child. For example, if their room is always a mess and it drives you to drink, don't throw negative, derogatory comments their way. Simply arrange to meet with them to set up a contract, and put consequences into place. However, you may need to pick your battles. If your preteen or teen leaves their room a mess, and it is only an irritant for you, you might want to set up a contract simply for them to keep their door closed so you don't have to trip over the spillage oozing out into the hall. For many teens, one of the symbols of independence is a messy room : *my* room, *my* mess. There may be other things far more important between you and your child that need to be addressed first.

Tip: As you problem solve with your child regarding unwanted behaviors, and you keep the energy positive, they will come to trust that you will remain calm when they "blow it" in life. The potential for them to come to you with serious life problems now increases, and you will be in a position to be a very powerful guide. A once negative cycle, this can now become a very rich positive relationship.

Tip #2: If a negative cycle has become too entrenched and you are unable to unravel it, this is the time to move it to a third party. Private or School Counselors who focus on parenting issues can help tremendously. However, don't wait. If the cycle becomes too entrenched, it can create complexes (refer to the Complexes Are The Pits) which can skew either or both of your perspectives for years to come. This, then, can create a potentially very difficult relationship between you and your child through their adulthood.

SECTION IV

THE TEEN FACTOR

TEEN PREJUDICE

As your child approaches the teen years, be aware of the prejudices you and your child may encounter. Friends and acquaintances who once responded positively to your child, may all of a sudden, upon hearing or recognizing that your child is about to become a teenager, start addressing you, in *front* of your child, as if you are about to become a victim of some horrendous cult. Be prepared for this now so if you do encounter this kind of discrimination you will know how to handle it. For example, if someone comes up to you and offers you sympathy because you are about to become a parent of a teen, you need to align with your child in that moment and not with the person who is, in essence, asking you to betray your child. This is the moment for you to step up to the plate and say something like, " I love teenagers. I can't wait until she/he becomes a teen." As you make your statement, smile at your child and put your arm around them. You may leave the other person blustering, but your child will recognize the powerful stance you have just taken, which is, *"I choose my child.* I choose my child over your prejudice and fear. I choose my child over *my* apprehension about the teen years. I choose my child despite the fact that I have just broken out in a cold sweat and have an urge to get down on my knees to pray for smooth sailing through the teenage years."

If you collude with the person offering sympathy, you have just left your child stranded, alone, and feeling like there is something wrong with them. They will understand that you crossed a line into another world that not only leaves them behind, but views them negatively. It would be the first step in their need to turn away from you to find their acceptance elsewhere.

Tip: The teenage years are wonderful years of idealism, enthusiasm, wit, and peels of laughter. If you align with your teen child rather than the prejudice about teens, you will be showered with these positive attributes. If you align with the prejudices instead of your child, you will become all too familiar with the absence of these attributes.

THE PRECARIOUS PEDESTAL

W hen your children are young, they may not recognize a double standard. For example, if you get furious at your children if they lie to you, they probably won't recognize that if you tell your friend she looks wonderful in her God-awful-dress, that you have just hedged on the truth a bit (possibly quite a bit, depending on the dress). However, as your children reach the teen years, they make a cognitive leap, and their brains which, hopefully, haven't yet been damaged by alcohol, smoking, stress, and, of course, aging, are on full alert and miss *nothing*. Couple this with the fact that teens are idealists, and hence, have a mad passion for fairness, know that whatever you exact from your teens, they will exact from you, pound for pound.

If lying is where you draw your line in the sand for your children, then be prepared, if your teen is listening, to tell your friend that her dress is ghastly, or more tact-fully, that it is your friend's opinion that counts and not yours (which, of course, your friend will immediately translate to mean that her dress *is* ghastly).

Remember that to an idealist, hypocrisy is a spear through the spleen. If you place yourself in a situation where you appear hypocritical, your teen will start tak-ing pot shots at the pedestal they placed you on when they were younger. While most adults feel justified in telling a few tall tales in "gray" situational areas, their teens will show them no mercy and will take no prison-ers. The more double standards there are, the more pre-carious the pedestal becomes, until the parent falls hard and swift and the teen turns to other teens to find a new leader. Remember, teens are idealistic *and* egocentric; a deadly combination when directed toward someone they feel just threw another spear through their spleen.

Tip: If you are graceful with your child when they tumble into touchy situations, they will be equally graceful with you when you do so, also. If you stay in your heart while you parent your child, your child has the ability to stay in their heart as they are par-ented. This becomes the positive standard by which the relationship between parent and child flourishes.

RUDENESS AS A RITUAL

If you have had a great relationship with your child and as they approach the preteen or teen years they begin to act rude, this could be a case of a self-induced ritual. In other words, if the relationship between you two has been sailing smoothly, but all of a sudden your child adopts a rude attitude, this might be their unspoken, and yet rather outspoken, demonstration of the self acknowledgement that they are indeed a teen. For in the homes of many of their friends, if relationships between child and parent have been strained, this is the time of life that children speak up; and they tend to do so with a sharp tongue. Many teens adopt this attitude because of a perceived discrepancy between what the parent is teaching and what the parent is doing. However, other teens or preteens who stumble upon these rude interchanges between their friends and parents, sometimes assume that this is happening because this is how teens express themselves. In other words, they develop the misconception that if you are a teen, you must speak rudely to parents/adults. Hence, if your child is stepping into "Teen-Dom," they will look toward the behaviors of other teens to define what it is like to be a teen. If they witness rude behavior, they now have a working model for how teens behave.

There are too few rituals for our children, especially as they enter puberty and the teen years. Positive rituals need to be created and implemented as teens begin this huge passage, which could replace the messy rooms, rude behavior, cigarettes, alcohol and drug experimentation that teens come up with out of desperation. The rituals should be geared to usher the teens, with dignity, through the entryway of this passage; to bestow upon them, among other things, their new status as role models for the younger set. In many schools this is being accomplished in the peer counseling programs, where teens learn how to help their friends and younger children who are experiencing problems. This raises the self-esteem of the teens, gives them a sense of direction and accomplishment, and makes them feel grown up in positive ways. It also gives them the tools and wisdom to help themselves and others, and awakens their sense of self and the impact they can have on others; as role models, as helpers, as teachers.

At home, you can create your own rituals. For example, when your daughter starts her menstrual cycle (you wouldn't need to announce to the family that she started her period, just that she is growing up; however, if this causes embarrassment or distress for you daughter, then perhaps the ritual could be when she enters the 6th or 7th grade) or when your son's voice begins to deepen or facial hair begins to develop (or when he enters the 6th or 7th grade) you could make a special dinner in their honor with the whole family in attendance, and give a special gift; especially the gift of honor and dignity, and ask them what new responsibility they feel ready for. In the weeks that follow, this would be a good time to introduce them into some of the age appropriate wisdom ways that you have discovered, about life, about relationships, about cause and effect.

Meanwhile, back at the ranch, if you have a preteen or teen that is all of a sudden starting to shoot rude comments or attitudes your way, you can sit down with them and explain the difficulty for you to remain sweet while having missiles fired your way. You can explain to them that there is something that humans do called *matching*. If they continue to fire missiles your way, the natural human response will be to match the energy, and fire a missile back of your own. When they realize that this is a two-way street and that it will be very difficult for them to have a wonderful relationship with you, while firing at you at every turn, they will most likely opt for the loving relationship they have always counted on. However, if there are underlying issues between you and your child, the rudeness probably won't disappear until the issues are cleared up.

> **Tip:** Our children need positive rituals in place as they enter the passage of young adulthood. Without the positive rituals, they are reduced to creating their own or emulating those negative ones already in place.

CONFOUNDED CURFEWS

Setting curfew for teens can be slippery. It takes the strength of a lion and the sweetness of a lamb to be able to set the boundary *and* satisfy your teen's sense of fair play. If they sniff any potential hoop-setting or uncertainty on your part, they will attempt to badger you to death in the hopes of wearing you down to a frazzle. Let's look at a dialogue designed to wear *them* down and appeal to their sense of fairness:

Teen: I think I should be allowed to stay out until midnight on Friday and Saturday nights.

Parent: I'm not comfortable changing your curfew at this time. 11:00 is my limit.

Teen: But everyone else gets to stay out past midnight!

Parent: I hear what you are saying, however, I'm not willing to risk your safety.

Teen: It's not risky to stay out until midnight! You are over protective!

Parent: Thank you. Just doing my job.

Teen: This is not fair!! I'll be fine.

Parent: That's very possibly true. However, I'll be a basket case every minute after 11:00, because I will be imagining very scary things happening to you.

Teen: You don't trust me.

Parent: Of course I trust you. What I don't trust is circumstance. There are some strange people out there, and if my gut says you aren't safe after 11:00 then you need to be in by 11:00.

Teen: Come on! That's not fair! How can I argue with your gut?

Parent: You can't. My gut and I are crazy about you, and it is our job to keep you safe.

Teen: Mom!!! Or Dad!!!!

Parent: Ask me again next year at this time. You will be older and I will have a year to see that you made it home safely on the weekends. In the meantime, when you get home at 11:00 on the dot, we can have some popcorn and play cards, which of course, I will win, hands down!

Teen: No way will you win! I always win!

Parent: We'll see.

Nicely done, Parent; and a nice face-saving gesture, too. (When you moved the focus to who will win at playing cards, your teen had a graceful "out"). Your teen learned a few things from this exchange:

- You set boundaries because you love your teen not because you like to see him/her jump through hoops.

- When you and your gut are aligned, you are immovable.

- You allow discussion; your teen gets to say his/her piece, and you get another chance to let your teen know how much they mean to you.

- There is life after curfew; popcorn, card games, a movie. Your teen may prefer their friends' company on a Friday or Saturday night, but coming home to some fun takes the sting out of having to leave their friends. If they are allowed to bring a friend or two home with them at curfew to spend the night, that is another great healing balm for the little stinging wound.

Tip: It is always handy if you are up waiting for your teen when they get home. It's hard to leave friends and come home to a dark and quiet house. However, if someone is waiting up for them, then they get to relay the exciting part of the evening, if you have (hopefully) established that kind of openness. You also get to make sure your teen is safe, on time, and sober. If you can make it somewhat festive when they return, then the arriving home feels like *a coming home*, and you get to welcome your teen back into the fold.

SECTION V

DEEPER WATERS

THE DIALOGUE OF BEHAVIOR
AND SYMPTOM

It is well known that when people get too stressed, the overwhelm they experience starts to surface in their behavior and/or in symptom. For example, irritability, fatigue, headaches, sleep disturbance, and ulcers are just some of the ways the mind/body dialogues (expresses itself) when under too much pressure. Old patterns are more likely to have their way, as well, as one goes into survival mode just to get through the day. As the mind and body take a beating, the unconscious realm gains more power.

Children, too, when they are stressed, frightened, or feel boxed in a corner, will shift their behavior accordingly, and if they find no relief from the mounting pressure, symptoms will begin to surface.

If children are misbehaving, a question you can ask yourself is, "What are they trying to tell me?" For example, if a compliant child suddenly balks or displays a bout of anger, something might be up. If this new behavior increases, then something indeed may be wrong. If a loquacious child is quiet for too long, as much as you may be thrilled with the sudden reprieve, you'll soon need to find out if something has happened.

When a child shifts behavior and you ask them if everything is alright, rather than reacting immediately to the unwanted behavior, the opportunity is there to sleuth out the potential problem underlying the behavior, rather than getting distracted by the behavior itself and thereby accidentally glossing over the original concern. A glossed over concern can get lost and buried if a struggle for compliance ensues, which could trigger more acting out on the child's part. If the initial problem remains undiscovered and the relationship between parent and child becomes strained, the sense of overwhelm for the child and the frustration for the parent could launch the relationship into a negative cycle. The problem, then, could get relegated to the sandy bottom of the child's psyche, sending out vague, undecipherable blips through the waves.

Some of the symptoms children display when their world is spinning out of control are headaches, stomach aches, intestinal problems, changes in sleeping patterns, appetite shifts, and nightmares. If the stress is traumatic enough, little ones can regress and thereby begin to wet and/or soil their pants. They might become clingy and their thumbs might pop back into their mouths. They may all of a sudden break out into baby talk. They may not want to leave you for fear that something will happen to you or to their way of life as they know it, while they are at day care or at school.

When children regress this is indicative of an unconscious attempt on the part of the child to go back to an earlier time when things weren't so stressful. For little ones, this could mean when they were toddlers, or even infants.

As children get older, their dialogue of overwhelm gets more extensive, and in addition to some of the physical symptoms already discussed, they may start acting sullen, withdrawn, non-compliant, angry, insolent, tearful, or paradoxically, turn into perfectionists in an attempt to keep rigid control over their lives. If teens and preteens have experienced loss and trauma, they may start to wear darker clothes, listen to depressing music, write dark poetry, display bouts of rage, start cutting themselves, quit organizations they used to be interested in, for example, sports; engage in drug use or abuse alcohol, change to peer groups that reflect their current psychic state, experience a drop in grades, become truant, and may begin to write or speak of death.

If your teen has shifted to darker clothes, this in itself, is not necessarily a cause for alarm; but if other indicators of depression are present, or other symptoms of overwhelm, then the darker clothes may be part of the dialogue of overwhelm or depression.

If your child exhibits this melancholy trend, and *over-dresses*, for example, wears clothes with long sleeves and long pants even in the hot weather, and if you realize that you haven't seen your child's limbs for a very long time, it could be an indicator that your teen is cutting their arms or legs with knives or other sharp objects, to relieve the overwhelming stress and pressure that is building in their life. Unfortunately, cutting oneself has become one of the responses to trauma and overwhelm in the teen world.

If you see that your teen's life is taking a downward spiral, and you notice that they overdress, and you fear they may be cutting, you can ask to see their arms; if you feel they would balk and refuse the request, you can get creative, and, for example, buy them a new top or shirt and ask them to model it. If they refuse to show you their arms or legs, or they refuse to model the new apparel, they may very well be hiding cut marks from you. Teens feel great shame when their parents discover that they cut, and anxiety is at peak levels as they worry that their parents will be traumatized if they find out. Their worry is valid; it is extremely traumatizing to think your child might be cutting.

If your child is taking a downward spin, don't hesitate to get them into counseling. This includes the little ones with persistent behavioral changes and physical symptoms, and of course, any child who displays symptoms of depression, cutting, or drug/alcohol abuse (Please refer to Symptoms of Depression/Suicidal Thinking). If money is an issue regarding counseling, a good first step is seeking help from the School Counselor. If your child makes suicidal statements, however, get them help **now**. If you can't get them into counseling immediately, you can take them to the emergency room of your local hospital to have them assessed or call the county Behavior Health (Mental Health) system's 24 hour hot line so you can speak with a therapist regarding your concerns.

Tip: Let your children know, starting from when they are little, that they can tell you anything; that you can handle anything they have to tell you. Sometimes children won't share a trauma because they have heard their parent say on occasion, "I can't take any more" when life has their parent up against the wall. Your children are listening to you, so this is an opportunity for you to reinforce to them all through their lives that you can take it; that you are able to help shoulder whatever emotional trauma comes their way.

WARNING SIGNS OF DEPRESSION/SUICIDAL THINKING

You can find many warning signs for depression listed on the internet, under *Depression*, *Signs of Depression*, *Warning Signs of Depression*, etc., and in specific books on the subject. There are many warning signs and when linked together in increasing numbers, they raise the risk factor for the presence of depression and, therefore, possibly for suicidal thinking. Obviously the more stressors or losses your child is burdened with, the higher the risk for depression. The more warning signs that apply, the greater the indication that depression is present. Some of these warning signs, when standing alone, may not point toward depression, for example, frequent complaints of boredom, or wearing dark colors, however, some warning signs carry more weight, and can stand alone. The more warning signs that are linked together, the greater the chance that your child is suffering from depression. However, as children enter the gateway into puberty, they may naturally start to sleep more, become voracious eaters (boys) or curb their diet (girls), and become irritable due to hormonal changes or due to the *"ritual of rudeness."* These signs don't *necessarily* point to depression but if you are worried about your child or if your child is burdened with significant stressors and/or other warning signs are present, then they will need to get into counseling to rule out or deal with the depression.

Not all people who are depressed consider suicide, due to their resilient nature, however, others consider suicide at an alarming rate when yet another loss or disappointing event sends them spiraling into a sea of hopelessness.

Listed below are many, but not all, of the warning signs for depression. One asterisk (*) indicates warning signs for depression and possible suicidal thinking. Two asterisks (**) indicates that suicidal thinking is, or most likely is, present. If you worry that your child is depressed, get them into private counseling or into your School Counselor. Many times children do not wish to burden their parents with their feelings of sadness or hopelessness, and so parents are unaware of the severity of the problem, or that the problem even exists. If you worry that your child is feeling suicidal, you need to get them help immediately. If you can't get them into counseling immediately, you can call the toll free number of Behavioral Health's (Mental Health) Crisis Line (which is listed in the phone book) for an assessment, or you can go to the emergency room of your local hospital for an assessment, or if you feel that your child is in imminent danger, call 911.

Warning signs of depression and suicidal thinking:

- If your child is burdened with significant stressors (the greater the number of stressors the greater the risk for depression). *Some* examples of significant stressors are: domestic violence in the home, drug/alcohol abuse in the home, divorce in the family, blended families, death of a loved one, exclusion from a peer group, romantic breakup, death of a beloved pet, suicide of a peer, moving to a new town or school, or an absentee parent.

- Always seems exhausted or develops insomnia.

- Loss of appetite or "emotional" overeating.

- Develops headaches, stomachaches, intestinal problems, or other physical symptoms.

- Seems irritable a lot of the time.

- Loss of interest in favorite activities.

- Grades start to plummet.

- Behavior shifts.

- Becomes dulled out or lethargic.

- Neglects personal appearance.

- Has bouts of sadness.

- Starts to wear black clothing or overdresses.

- Becomes anxious

- Develops panic attacks

- Becomes accident prone.

- Expresses hopeless, helpless, cynical or self-critical thinking.

- Expresses concern that nobody cares.

- Displays bouts of rage.

- Becomes careless about her/his own safety.

- Shows signs of substance abuse.

- Relationships with family or friends start to flounder.

- Self-esteem starts to plummet.

- Isolates from friends and family.

•• Listens to music that focuses on death/suicide.

•• Writes prose or poetry about death; writes *DEATH* on binder or papers.

•• Starts cutting themselves or other self-inflicted injuries.

•• Makes statements such as, "I wish I could die," or "I don't want to live anymore."

•• Threatens to hurt or kill self.

•• Makes indirect statements, such as, "No one would care if I die" or " I just can't take it anymore."

•• Gives away favorite belongings.

•• Suddenly becomes extremely cheerful during a bout of depression (unless the initial reason for the depression has been resolved, i.e., Mom and Dad got back together or child is eligible to play sports again, etc.). The warning here is that some people who feel suicidal become extremely cheerful when they come up with a suicide plan, and feel their suffering is about to be over.

•• Creates suicide notes.

> **Tip:** Take note of the stressors and possible warning signs for depression in your child's life. If you are worried about your child, get them into counseling. It's always better to be on the safe side. Remember that when someone is overburdened, it doesn't take a huge loss to flatten them.

THE RAVAGES OF DOMESTIC
VIOLENCE

If you find yourself out of control at times, falling prey to an overwhelming rage, and directing that rage physically or mentally onto your spouse/partner and/or children, you need to get help immediately. If you refer to Taken Hostage and Complexes Are the Pits you will start to understand what is happening to you. Chances are that you grew up in a violent household, and/or you are having feelings of unworthiness or impotent rage on the job (or because there is no job), and in your dealings with people and life in general. There is help for you and your family, however, you must find a therapist immediately before you inflict any more damage. Some Domestic Violence (D.V.) Programs have free counseling for the whole family; if counseling is not available, they will know who to refer you to. Admittedly, in some families of domestic violence, both spouses/partners are inflicting emotional and physical pain onto each other, with one person usually getting more wounded than the other in the fracas. In either event, there are therapists available either through the D.V. Programs or through a referral, and they are trained in this field. All you need to do is call and ask for help. The toll free phone numbers for the domestic violence shelters/programs are in the phone book. If you call and say something like, "My family needs help," they will be all over it. There is nothing more heartening than someone who wants to make positive changes. If you worry, in the interim, that you may hurt any family member, before or during therapy, you will need to remove yourself from your home (if you are hurting your children, Child Protective Services may mandate that you remove yourself from the home) and get a temporary apartment or stay with a friend or relative, in order to protect your loved ones. What a loving act that will be, insuring your family's safety. Once your whole family begins therapy and you (and your partner if they are also violent) have shifted the abusive patterning, only then will it be safe for you to return home; your therapist will let you know when and if you are ready.

If you are the *victim* of domestic violence, you need to seek help immediately. The situation is not likely going to get better; in all probability, it's only going to get worse for you as well as for the whole family unless you all receive therapy. Even then, there are no guarantees that the abuser will be able to shift his or her violent patterning. It will take dedication on his/her part, and yours, as well. There are toll free hot-line phone numbers listed in the phone book for the domestic violence shelters which provide confidential assistance, crisis plans, legal advice, and shelter if you are in danger. The phone number is usually listed in the very front of the phone book under Community Service Numbers. The best thing of course, would be for the whole family to get into therapy, once you and the children are out of danger; however, if you feel your spouse/partner would shun help or if the situation is deadly, you and the children need to get help and/or get to a safe place, regardless. If you or your children are living in a dangerous situation, the domestic violence team can help get you all to safety. Call 911 if you are in imminent danger. Their response is immediate, and they can take you and the children to the shelter.

Let's now look at the effects of domestic violence on the children. Please refer to the Taken Hostage section of the book to give you a general understanding of how patterning works. Having read the section you can now recognize how patterns are introjected into the psyche.

Children of domestic violence are impacted in many ways. Of course, if *they* are being physically assaulted, not only are they in bodily danger, but the patterning to repeat the cycle, either as the perpetrator or the victim, is being hammered into them. Sexual assault, also, can occur in families of domestic violence, as once one disregards the physical sanctum of a loved one's body, the violation can take many forms. Not only does this create patterning around the theme of sexual abuse in the psyches of the children, but as teenagers, they will have a high propensity for depression, cutting, drug and alcohol abuse, mental/emotional instability, and suicidal thinking.

If children are the victims of emotional abuse, those patterns are also being implanted in their tender psyches, and when they grow up the chances of them unconsciously selecting a partner that will complete the abusive cycle, are great.

When children are born into a home of physical, sexual, or emotional abuse, the shining light of their pure potential is thwarted and rerouted into that of survival. This is also true even if the children are not physically, sexually, or mentally abused; having their parents/caregivers caught up in a cycle of violence is enough to do the trick.

If the children see, hear, know of, or worry about the physical or emotional violence of their guardians, their immediate and future well being is impacted:

- They may not be able to concentrate in school.

- They may be too afraid to sleep, or conversely, sleep too much in an attempt to escape.

- They may be frightened to leave home for fear of what might happen while they are away.

- They may live in terror that one or both of their parents might get maimed or killed.

- They may "walk on eggshells" or turn into little perfectionists with the hope that the violence won't be turned on them.

- They may start "identifying with the aggressor" in an unconscious attempt to thwart any potential violence towards them. If they do identify with the aggressor, they may adopt the same abusive behaviors as the perpetrator.

- They may feel shame and guilt for not being able to stop the violence.

- They may take on the role of the protector and pit themselves against one parent.

- They may regress in an unconscious attempt to feel safe.

- They may develop physical symptoms (please refer The Dialogue of Behavior and Symptom).

- They may become hyper-vigilant.

- Their startle reflex may become acute.

- They may become accident prone and careless about their own safety.

- They may view the world in general as an unsafe place.

These are just some of the ways children respond to domestic violence. The longer they are exposed to the violence (not just witnessing the violence, but also worrying about the violence) the deeper the wounding, the stronger the patterning to repeat the cycle when they grow up, and the more entrenched the inner conflict and chaos becomes as it grapples within their psyches. The sooner the children are removed from this cycle, the better chance they have for recovery.

Tip: If you find yourself in a domestic violence situation, get help immediately. The longer it goes on, the higher the risks are for the whole family. The person who is violent usually feels remorse for what he/she has done and may plead for forgiveness. You need to recognize that this is part of the cycle of violence. Call the toll free hot line for Domestic Violence. They will give you all of the information and statistics regarding the cycle of violence. Become informed and get the help you need. Remember, your children's personalities and psyches are being formed around that violence. And don't forget; your children need you whole, healthy, and alive.

SECTION VI

COMING UP FOR AIR

SCARY MOVIES/ SCARY NEWS

While scary movies can be entertaining and hype up the body with adrenaline, provide sick humor if it is a "B" horror flick, and give one substantial relief when the lights go up, there is something at play here that needs to be addressed. The scary images and scenes that are projected onto the screen become options for the psyche to use when a person is later stressed, anxious, or frightened. If the movie is scary enough, this in itself will trigger a nightmare using the images just seen on the screen. However, the images are stored in the psyche and can resurface as nightmare material, weeks, months, and even years down the road. The more scary movies one views, the more images that are stored; the more frightening the movie, the more frightening the potential nightmare.

Children have access to a wide variety of scary movies with cable and satellite TV. While they may tell you they won't get scared, and beg to watch the movies, you need to know that the images will be stored in their little psyches for later fodder to fuel their dream world when they are feeling anxious or frightened. For the young ones, the images viewed are much more frightening and since they see the world in a more concrete fashion, the images are all the more real. So if your child sees a terrifying movie, the potential for the terrifying figures to come to life in your child's dreamscape is significant.

The news on TV is equally, if not more, frightening to children as scary movies are. At least in scary movies there is usually someone telling them that the images they are seeing are not real. Since children are concrete thinkers this is not totally reassuring, however, regarding the news, no one is even attempting to tell them this is not real. Since the media focuses on the Shocking and the Violent, children and adults, alike, hear hour after hour of shocking and violent news. There are always plenty of traumatic happenings across the globe, which, when singled out and gathered up, gives a skewed view of reality. What is lacking in the global news are all the gentle day to day kindnesses, the kitties rescued from the trees, sweet babies taking their first step, a highlight of lovers saying their wedding vows, etc. However, the networks know that audiences are transfixed by disastrous news and so the skewed reality is what is portrayed.

Watching the nightly news has many repercussions:

- Distressing and frightening news, of course, causes distress and fear for its viewers. If watched just before bedtime, this causes anxious and fearful dreams, and you guessed it, the terrifying images from scary movies are potentially released in proportion to the caliber of fear generated by the news.

- Children don't see as holistically as their parents and aren't as aware of the goodness happening around the globe, hence, they buy into the portrayed skewed reality.

- The constant taking in of shocking and violent data creates a sense of doom in adults and children, alike. Many preteens and teens become heavily burdened by this sense of doom and become depressed as a sense of helplessness cripples them.

- When there is a crisis shown on the media, all are transfixed in horror, as the same images are hammered again and again into the collective audience. The body and psyche are repeatedly traumatized by the images and the body responds by overloading chemicals into its system, such as adrenaline, as it goes into "fight or flight" each time the media sequences are repeated. Remember, your children take their cues from you; if you, their protectors, are frightened and distressed, they will be diving for cover, sure that the *sky is falling.*

- If people's lives are dismal, and they feel hopeless and unloved, and are hammered nightly by violent news, and if they have a fragile psyche, they could ultimately crack and add to the cycle of violence. The more violence shown through the media, the more potential for violence to occur.

Tip: If you need a dose of nightly news, you could look it up on your computer well before bedtime. In this way, your children won't be exposed to the nightly trauma/drama, and you get to select what you wish to be informed about. Doing it well before bedtime reduces your own risk of taking the anxiety to bed with you. In place of nightly TV, try board games with your children. They will be thrilled, the family will have a sense of unity, and all will go to bed dreaming innocuously of Chutes and Ladders.

Tip #2: Rent or watch movies at home that have redemptive, heartwarming themes. You and your children need these positive messages for your psyches to balance out the gloom and doom of pessimistic news, pessimistic views, disappointments, loss, and daily stress. You will also not be adding to the gene pool of terrifying psychic images for yourself or your children.

CHOICES, CHOICES, CHOICES

Giving your children choices is very important for their growth, maturity, sense of self, not to mention that it makes life *much* easier for you! Let's use the example of getting your little ones to bed at night (parenting technique inspired by "Parenting With Love And Logic," by Foster Cline & Jim Fay) to illustrate the benefits of choices:

- It moves your children into action: "It's almost time for bed. Do you want to wear superman or batman pajamas?" As they yell, "batman!!" they are a step closer to bed.

- It avoids the power play: If you simply say "it's time for bed. Go!" They will likely stall, pout, throw a fit, or if too defeated to put up a fight, go to bed

111

teary eyed or at least dejectedly, and then may call out incessantly for water, for potty, or wander to your bed during the night claiming bad dreams or a stomachache.

- It empowers them. When choices are introduced at a young age, children get used to thinking, "what *is* it that I want?" If choices are not introduced, children can become overly compliant or oppositional. If they become overly compliant they are at a greater risk to succumb to peer pressure. If they become oppositional, it sets up a negative cycle between you and your child. With choices, children feel they have a say in their own lives. This is a good thing as long as they also have boundaries and guide-lines.

When your children are very young, then every step of the way toward bedtime can be guided with choices, for example: "Do you need to go potty before you brush your teeth?" The answer is either yes or no. If yes, they go potty and then are ready for the teeth brushing. If no, then the teeth brushing comes first, and they now have been prompted to know that potty is coming next. Then, for the teeth brushing, do they want this tooth paste or that one? Then the gallop toward bed, with, "let's pick out a book so I can read you a story. Do you want this story or that one?" You have just guided your child to bed with a smooth and happy transition. As you read to them, they have the luxury of becoming drowsy to the rhythm of your voice; to the sweet fantasy of the story. They have you close by them and get to snuggle. It is a beautiful way to let your child drift into the unconscious realm; a safe passage into the vulnerable dreamscape.

With choices in place and the promise of snuggles and a bed-time story, this sets up each night as not only a smooth transition for both of you, but a happy event.

Of course choices work in all action. Getting dressed for school or getting homework done, "Do you want to do your homework before we go to the park or afterwards?" Most likely they will choose the park first, but they already know that when they get back, homework is next on the list.

The "Love and Logic" series by Jim Fay (the "choices" guru) goes into great depth regarding choices and is a wonderful resource. You can find these books at most book stores and at loveandlogic.com. Another great resource is, "Winning at Parenting Without Beating Your Kids." The author, Barbara Coloroso, talks about the need to give more choices, not less, to your children as they grow older, so that by the time they leave home at age 18, they understand cause and effect, and have access to their inner voice which will guide their choices. Winning at Parenting is available on DVD and CD; Ms. Coloroso wrote a new best selling book based the DVD of Winning at Parenting, which is called "Kids Are Worth It." *Winning at Parenting* and *Kids Are Worth It*, as well as other parenting books Ms. Coloroso has written, are available on her website: kidsareworthit.com., as well as in the major book stores and Amazon.com

Barbara Coloroso has another great tip in *Winning at Parenting*. When your child asks you a question, say "yes" as much as you can. For example, if your child asks for a cookie and dinner is an hour away, say "Yes! You can have a cookie after dinner." Or if your child asks if a friend can spend the night, say, "Yes! This weekend will be a good time." In this way, your child gets a *directional* green light most of the time, and when you say "NO" they will pay attention. And there are times when you will have to say no, and when you say it, it will carry an impact. For example, "Can I spend the night with Joe (the school drug dealer)?" The answer: "NO." Your child will feel the energy of the stop sign, for it's an unusual event in their lives. If they hear *no* all of the time: "No, you can't have a cookie… no you can't have your friend over…no you can't watch your program…no you can't sleep over at Joe's, the school drug dealer…it just becomes another "no" event.

Tip: Choices not only guide your child smoothly toward action, but also empower them along the way as they learn that their voice counts. As they get used to small day to day decisions, it paves the way for them to be able to make wise decisions in delicate situations when they are older.

OUT COMPLAINING THE COMPLAINERS

When Children complain about their chores, homework, or having to get up early, etc., and if they have already heard the explanations about the benefits or reasons for doing these "arduous" tasks, more explanations will only reinforce the frustrating cycle of their complaints and your explanations.

What *can* stop their complaining is the validation of their perspective and at the same time, shifting the energy by complaining with them. This tactic seems to satisfy the little magpies and seems to stop them cold. In fact, they seem to get a perverse delight in having the complaint department shift from their shoulders to yours.

For example, if your child is complaining about their homework, you can say something like, "No!!! No more homework!! I can't stand it! It messes up the dining table and you sit there for hours!" If you use a dramatic and funny voice, they will usually turn the situation around immediately and tell you they have *lots* of homework, and immediately dig it out and giggle while you moan about it. When they ask for help, roll your eyes and give them the crazy horse eye. If all works out well, you will have them in stitches, the homework will get done, and they will prance away excited that you are the one who now gripes about their homework.

If the little sweethearts complain about having to go to school, you can say, "I know how you feel! *I* don't want to go to work. I don't! You can't make me!!" They will laugh and probably tell you that you have to go to work, which then you can resign to your fate with some moans. Or, if they tell you don't have to go to work, that you should all stay home, you can muse out loud with lots of sighs about why you probably should show up for work. Since you are sharing the burden about having to do things you don't want to do, they will most probably go off to school, pleased that someone feels the same way that they do. It's more about validation than anything else.

It works the same with chores. If they moan about taking out the garbage, you can say something like, "Tell me about it! I don't ever want to clean the kitchen again. I hate it. That's all I ever do!" They will probably tell you that you must clean the kitchen, or they might even ask if you need help. But they won't feel so badly about having to do things they don't want to do, when they know they aren't the only ones who feel that way.

> **Tip:** Humor, dramatics, and validation go a long way. A seemingly endless cycle of complaints can turn around in a moment into laughter, which greases the wheel of positive action.

THINGS TO KEEP IN MIND

- Remember to be consistent. Your children will badger you to death if you say, "Just this once." When you aren't consistent, your children will know that there is a soft spot to a particular rule, and they will try umpteen times to find that soft spot again, before they give up. This will be crazy making for you as well as for them. Children need boundaries; they need to know what to expect and what is expected of them.

- A little grace goes a long way. Everyone has accidents, whether it is spilling the milk, dropping a vase, or backing in to another car. If you have ever had anyone laugh off one of your mistakes or accidents, you know how wonderful it feels to be immediately forgiven. When you extend that kindness to your child, grace descends upon you both.

- Have fun with your children. Parenting can be tough. Relationships can be a struggle. You and your children need the good times to balance out the challenging times. Get silly. Laugh together. Surprise your children with popcorn parties, treasure hunts, fun excursions. Turn off the TV and play board games or Charades. Let your children and your inner child delight in each other.

- Remember, as you implement these teachings from Nitty Gritty Parenting, to be kind and loving to yourself. This is a wonderful thing that you are doing; searching for better ways to parent. It might take awhile before you get the hang of the new concepts. If you find that you have "stepped in it," try to figure out what went wrong, and then dust yourself off (and your children if they got splattered), and reorient yourself to the higher road. Good luck and God Bless.

Made in the USA
Charleston, SC
28 October 2010